This magical book of fun adventure belongs to

_____

To Cathy Youngs, thank you for your continued enthusiasm and support, and to all the little skiers skiing Taos Ski Valley, Taos, New Mexico.

- Sandy "Sam"

www.mascotbooks.com

Scooter the Purple Mogul Mouse

©2013 Sandra Newman. All Rights Reserved. No part of this publication may be reproduced, stored in a retrieval system or transmitted in any form by any means electronic, mechanical, or photocopying, recording or otherwise without the permission of the author.

For more information, please contact:

Van de Bogart
PUBLISHING

info@vb-publishing.com

20 Portsmouth Ave #41 - Stratham, NH 03885

Library of Congress Control Number: 2013952880

CPSIA Code: PRT1213A
ISBN-10: 1620865637
ISBN-13: 9781620865637

Printed in the United States

SCOOTER

The Purple Mogul Mouse

and All his Mogul Mouse Friends

Sandra Newman

illustrated by
Kellie Green

Sandra Newman

Let's read a story about my friends and me, Scooter!

There's Giggles who giggles all the time.

Aliea and Lauren, the twins who always wear blue.

Over there sitting on her tail, that's K-K-Katie!

Under the tree? Austin, he's always tripping over his tail.

And chasing the skier? That's Mosley.

See how quick he runs? He's always having so much fun.

Then there is me, Scooter, the best at scooting across ski trails.

Where do Mogul Mice live?

We live in ski areas all over the world

with our moms and dads, brothers and sisters,

aunts and uncles, cousins, and all our Mogul Mouse friends.

Our houses are moguls, those gigantic mounds of snow.

"The big bumpity-bumps," Giggles squeaks.

Just beware skiing the moguls,

you might be entering a Mogul Mouse Town.

For fun and games, Mogul Mice play with snowboarders and skiers.

So watch out when you ski the bumps and run over a mogul house.

If a Mogul Mouse tumbles out of bed and lands on his head,

and the dishes rattle and clang to the floor,

a Mogul Mouse will boldly head for the door,

chasing you through the bumps and trees for a free ride on your skis.

What do Mogul Mice look like?

We are so cuddly and cute,

with grape juice purple fur, shiny red noses,

and carrot stick orange eyes, so sparkly and bright.

"Our ears are perfectly-perfect, bubble-gum-popping-pink!"

Lauren excitedly explains.

Being a Mogul Mouse is so much fun!

We get to play in heaps of piled-up snow,

sliding and gliding into the moguls on our big fat tails.

Austin claims, "Our fluffy tails are ever so big. We use them for sleds.

And steering with the tip never fails."

K-K-Katie wants you to believe,
"Mogul Mice are magic."
Big people can't see Mogul Mice.
So when you ride the chairlift high in the sky,
try hard not to squirm like a worm.
Remember, make a wish
when you feel the swish of that big, fat magical tail.

Mogul Mice picnic high in the trees,
munching on nuts and berries, sipping Gooseberry Tea.
From this perch high above
we watch the skiers cruising around,
tossing snowballs when they fall down.
And when it snows ever so hard,
the Mogul Mice jump to the ground,
playing in the snowflakes floating down.

Our little skier friends gave us presents last year.
Candy cane striped slippers, so much fluffier than our tails.
We wear them everywhere, even to bed while resting our heads.
"We love our slippers," squeak the Mogul Mice
all over Mogul Mouse Town.

You might wonder, where do Mogul Mice go in the summer?

We tunnel underground in fields next to streams,

building houses of sticks, trees, and leaves.

We scurry about playing with our friends,

the bunnies, squirrels, and bees.

Traveling south we visit our cousin, Willie, the Mesa Mouse.

So when you rumble, tumble, and fall
skiing through the moguls and trees,
blame it on my friends and me, Scooter!
We are the Purple Mogul Mice,
chasing you through the bumps and the trees!

Remember Scooter's warning,

"Always wear your helmet

just in case you run into my friends and me!"

With your parents' permission,
contact Scooter and his buds at

scooter@scooterthepurplemogulmouse.com

About the Author

Sandra "Sam" Newman began skiing as a little girl in northern Maine. While teaching skiing for Taos Ski Valley's Children's Ski School in Taos, New Mexico, Sam began telling the funny, heartwarming legend of Scooter, a magical Purple Mogul Mouse who lives in ski moguls. Knowing that learning to ski can be very scary for children and adults, especially when bumps or moguls are seen and tried for the first time, she started to tell funny stories of Scooter and his friends. Her students insisted that the tale of Scooter, the Purple Mogul Mouse, become a book because they want to see the movie. When not writing, Sandy works as a corporate flight attendant and owns SN Design Co. You can contact her directly at sandy@vb-publishing.com if you have any questions about Scooter, his friends, and their upcoming adventures.

About the Illustrator

Kellie Green holds an Associate Degree in Art & Design and for the last two decades has worked as a logo and graphic art designer for small businesses and ministries. She resides in south central Pennsylvania, where she enjoys spending time with her family.

Other books written by Sandra Newman

Life & Times on Pleasant Pond

Scooter Meets a Stumbling, Bumbling Fly

Scooter Asks his Friends some Mogul Mouse Questions

1. Why are Mogul Mouse ears bubble-gum-popping-pink?

2. Why are Mogul Mouse eyes carrot stick orange?

3. Why do the Mogul Mice wear candy cane striped slippers?

4. Why are Mogul Mice grape juice purple?

5. Does Scooter have a girlfriend?

6. How big is a Mogul Mouse tail?

7. How big is a Mogul Mouse?

8. Do Mogul Mice have beds in their houses?

Scooter's Friends' Answers

1. Lauren's answer. "Because Giggles is always chewing pink bubble gum and popping bubbles!"

2. K-K-Katie's answer. "Because you eat carrots for your eyes, and they taste good."

3. Mosley wisely explains this one. "Last year, when Lauren and Aliea were sitting on a chairlift high in the sky, the little skiers sitting in the chair had red and white striped candy canes. Then, when our little skier friends wanted to give us presents last year because they thought our feet were cold, they knew we liked the colors of the candy canes. So…candy cane striped slippers! We never wore anything on our feet before our slippers. Now our feet are warm and cozy."

4. Giggle's likes this answer because it was her idea. "We are grape juice purple because the author likes the color dark purple and we are from her imagination. With her help, we make people have fun skiing and using their imaginations!"

5. Lauren likes this answer because it is her twin sister. "Aliea is Scooter's girlfriend!"

6. Since Austin is always sitting on his tail, he answers this one. "It's fluffy and long like a fox tail! It's a very comfy place to sit."

7. Aliea provides this answer. "That's a tough answer, Scooter. Maybe the tallest is this high?"

8. Scooter's answer. "Mogul Mice are part of your creative imagination. Your imagination creates us. Always remember, we only create happy, safe fun!"